Itchy Scritchy Scratchy Pants

Steve Smallman

Elina Ellis

LITTLE TIGER
LONDON

Five cold Vikings went out hiking,
Through a sudden snowstorm, wondering what to do.
Well, they'd got into a fight, had their undies set alight,
Now their pants were all in pieces and their bums were turning blue!

For Scarlet and Gabby (who cannot sit still!)

~ S S

For my favourite artist, Sasha Polivar

~ E E

LITTLE TIGER PRESS,
an imprint of the Little Tiger Group
1 Coda Studios, 189 Munster Road, London SW6 6AW
www.littletiger.co.uk
First published in Great Britain 2018

Text copyright © Steve Smallman 2018
Illustrations copyright © Elina Ellis 2018

Steve Smallman and Elina Ellis have asserted their rights
to be identified as the author and illustrator of this work under the
Copyright, Designs and Patents Act, 1988

ISBN 978-1-84869-941-0
Printed in China
LTP/1400/2187/0318
2 4 6 8 10 9 7 5 3 1

"My bottom's cold!" moaned Yop as they found a little shop;
A sign said 'Knitted Knickers' on the door.
But because it was so cold,
all the knickers had been sold,
And there wasn't any wool
to knit some more!

We're DOOMED!

But the knicker lady said, "At the summit of Mount Dread,
There's a yeti who's mysterious and clever.
So if you bring me a sack of the fur from off his back,
Then I'll knit you all the warmest knickers ever!"

BEST
KNITTED
KNICKERS

THE
KNICKER LADY
of the
MONTH

OUT OF
STOCK!

In the Forest of Despair
our brave Vikings met a bear,
Plus a pack of wolves
who rushed in to attack.

Harald gave the wolves a shock
with a well-aimed stinky sock,

And the bear hugged Grim . . .
but Grim just hugged him back!

Ahh! He wants a cuddle!

As the Vikings, out of breath,
rowed across the Sea of Death,
They were swallowed by a massive
monster trout!

So then Loggi
started

whacking i

and kicking it,

and smacking it,

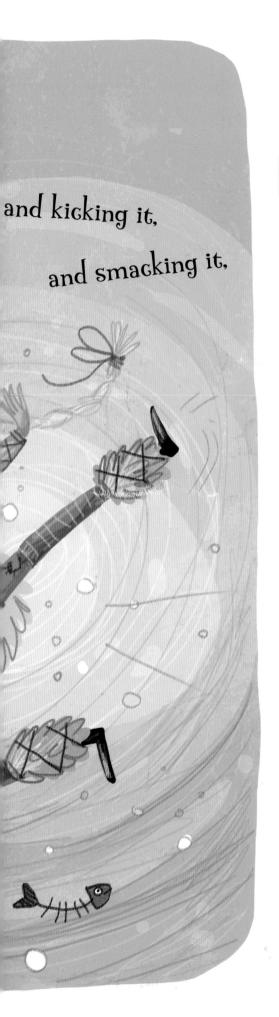

Until the fish felt sick
and spat them out!

Well, it's very hard to climb when you're covered in fish slime,
But at last they reached the summit of Mount Dread,
Where they found a fearsome beast (it was ten feet tall at least!)
And it opened up its massive mouth and said . . .

"Don't be worried, I won't eat you,
I am very pleased to meet you!
People hardly ever come up to my cave!"

Bushy Bigbeard gave a shout,
whipped his yeti clippers out,
And said, "Come on, gang,
let's give this guy a shave!"

Then their feet began to slide,
"Ooh be careful!" Yeti cried.
"If you fall into Lake Doom it won't be nice."

Well, they did fall in and when
the yeti pulled them out again
They were frozen into massive blocks of ice!

Then they heard a mighty roar and the frozen Vikings saw
A huge dragon who looked down at them and grinned,
"Viking lollies! Oh, how sweet! You look good enough to eat.
But I won't though, Vikings always give me wind!"

So the dragon thawed them out
with the fire from his snout,

And the yeti said, "I do not need a shave!
But if you want some yeti fluff,
    I've got masses of the stuff.
Look, I keep it down the back end of my cave!"

Five happy Vikings, all quite liking
Riding on a dragon to the Knitted Knickers shop;

And when their knickers had been knitted,
and they tried them and they fitted,
Then they paid the knicker lady
from the piggy bank of Yop!

Well, the knickers were so cosy that their cheeks went pink and rosy
Then, "MY BOTTOM'S GONE ALL OUGHY!" Harald cried.
And soon everyone was itching, jumping up and down and twitching
As their brand new pants had YETI FLEAS inside!